·PETER & the WOLF·

·PETER· & the WOLF·

Retold and Illustrated by
IAN BECK

Picture Corgi Books

Peter lived with his grandfather in a little wooden house at the edge of a great dark forest. Around their house was a garden and beyond the garden was a meadow.

Early one morning, Peter opened the garden gate and went out into the big green meadow.

High up in a tree sat a little bird, who was Peter's friend. 'All is quiet, all is quiet,' sang the bird. Just then, a fat white duck came waddling along. She was glad that Peter had left the gate open, and decided to go for a swim in the deep pond.

Seeing the duck, the little bird flew down from the tree and settled next to her on the grass. He looked her up and down. 'What kind of bird are *you* if you can't fly?' he said.

The duck just shook her feathers and said, 'What kind of bird are *you* if you can't swim?' and dived into the water.

Peter watched them as they argued and argued – the duck quacking in the pond, the little bird hopping round the edge.

Suddenly, something caught Peter's eye. It was a cat, creeping slowly towards them.

The cat was thinking, 'While the little bird is so busy arguing with that duck, I'll just grab him.' Stealthily she crept nearer and nearer on her soft, velvet paws . . .

'Look out!' shouted Peter. And the bird flew high into the tree, while the duck flapped and quacked at the cat from the middle of the pond. The cat walked round and round the tree and thought, 'Is it worth climbing up so high? By the time I get near the bird, he will have flown away.'

Just then, Grandfather came out of the house. He was angry that Peter had gone out into the meadow. 'It's a dangerous place, this. Suppose a wolf were to come out of the great dark forest. What would you do then, eh?'

Peter paid no attention to his grandfather's
words. Boys like *him* aren't afraid of wolves.
But Grandfather took Peter by the hand,
led him home and locked the garden gate.

No sooner had Peter gone, than a big grey wolf *did* come out of the forest!

In a flash, the cat climbed the tree. The duck quacked and flapped and jumped out of the pond. But no matter how hard the duck ran, she couldn't escape the wolf. With every step, he was getting nearer and nearer...

Finally, he caught her! And with one huge gulp, swallowed her!

Now this is how things were: the cat was sitting on one branch of the tree and the little bird on another (not too close to the cat) while the wolf walked round and round the tree, looking up at them with greedy eyes.

All this time, Peter, completely fearless, stood behind the closed gate, watching everything that was going on. He ran quickly into the house, fetched a strong rope and climbed the high stone wall.

One of the branches of the tree around which
the wolf was prowling stretched up over the wall.
Peter grabbed hold of the branch and climbed
on to the tree.

'Fly down and circle round the wolf's head,'
he said to the little bird. 'Only watch out that
he doesn't catch you!'

The little bird flew as close as he could, almost touching the wolf's head with his wings, while the wolf snapped angrily at him from this side and that.

How the bird worried the wolf and how the wolf wanted to catch him, but the little bird was too clever and the wolf simply couldn't do anything about it.

Meanwhile, Peter made a lasso out of the strong rope and, very carefully letting it down, he caught the wolf by the tail, and pulled with all his might.

Feeling himself caught, the wolf snarled and jumped wildly, trying to escape. But Peter had tied the other end of the rope to the tree and the wolf's jumping only made the rope round his tail tighter.

Just then, some hunters came out of the dark forest. They were following the wolf's trail in the snow, shooting their guns as they marched.

Peter, high in the tree, called out, 'Don't shoot! The little bird and I have caught the wolf. Now we can take him to the zoo.'

Imagine the triumphant procession ... Peter at the front, then the hunters leading the wolf, then Grandfather. And, right at the end, the cat. Grandfather shook his head. 'Ah it's all very well ... but what if Peter *hadn't* caught the wolf? What then, eh?'

Above them flew the little bird, singing happily, 'My, what brave fellows we are, Peter and I. Look what we've caught!'

And, if you listen *very* carefully you might hear the fat duck quacking inside the wolf because the wolf, in his hurry, had swallowed her whole!

Peter and the Wolf was composed by the great Russian composer Sergei Prokofiev (1891–1953) to introduce children to the instruments of the orchestra. Each character in the story is represented by a different instrument:

the Bird by the flute

the Duck by the oboe

the Cat by the clarinet

the Grandfather by the bassoon

the Wolf by the French horns

Peter by the strings

and the Hunters' guns by the drums

If you look carefully at each page of this book, you can spot the instruments as the different characters appear.

Also available by Ian Beck, and published by
Picture Corgi Books

THE TEDDY ROBBER
HUSH-A-BYE BABY
EMILY AND THE GOLDEN ACORN
TOM AND THE ISLAND OF DINOSAURS
THE OWL AND THE PUSSY-CAT